CLEMENTINE ROSE

and the Special Promise

Books by Jacqueline Harvey

CLEMENTINE ROSE

and the Special Promise

Jacqueline Harvey

RANDOM HOUSE AUSTRALIA

A Random House book
Published by Random House Australia Pty Ltd
Level 3, 100 Pacific Highway, North Sydney NSW 2060
www.randomhouse.com.au

Penguin
Random House
Australia

First published by Random House Australia in 2016

Random House Books is part of the Penguin Random House
group of companies whose addresses can be found at
global.penguinrandomhouse.com/offices.

National Library of Australia
Cataloguing-in-Publication Entry

Author: Jacqueline Harvey
Title: Clementine Rose and the special promise/Jacqueline Harvey
ISBN: 978 0 85798 786 0 (pbk)
Series: Harvey, Jacqueline. Clementine Rose; 11
Target audience: For primary school age
Subjects: Girls – Juvenile fiction.
          Friendship – Juvenile fiction.
Dewey number: A823.4

Cover and internal illustrations by J.Yi
Cover design and additional illustration by Leanne Beattie
Internal design by Midland Typesetters, Australia
Typeset in ITC Century 12.5/19 by Midland Typesetters, Australia
Printed in Australia by Griffin Press, an accredited ISO AS/NZS
14001:2004 Environmental Management System printer

Random House Australia uses papers that are natural, renewable and
recyclable products and made from wood grown in sustainable forests.
The logging and manufacturing processes are expected to conform to the
environmental regulations of the country of origin.

For Ian, whose special promise changed my life forever in the best possible way

SWEET GOODBYES

Clementine Rose pushed open the door to Pierre's Patisserie and was met with the mouth-watering aroma of freshly baked bread and sausage rolls. Digby Pertwhistle followed her and paused to breathe it in.

Clementine loved going to Pierre's. It had dainty white tables with bentwood chairs and a wall of black-and-white photographs of famous places in Paris. Among them was the Eiffel Tower and a huge cathedral called

1

Notre-Dame. Everything about the shop was pretty, right down to the swirly writing on the faded sign, and the crisp red aprons that Pierre and his wife, Odette, always wore.

Pierre had just been putting the finishing touches to a birthday cake when he turned to see who had come in. 'Good afternoon, Clementine! Good afternoon, Monsieur Digby!' he said, his eyes crinkling as he smiled.

'Good afternoon, Pierre,' Digby replied with a nod of his head.

'*Bonjour*, Pierre,' Clementine said, making sure to get the pronunciation right. 'Sophie has been teaching me some French words.'

Sophie Rousseau was Pierre's daughter and Clementine's best friend. They'd known one another since they were babies.

'I can 'ear that. For a second there I thought you were French!' Pierre grinned and rubbed his hands together. 'Now, what can I get for you today?'

Clementine peered into the long glass cabinet at the delicious array of treats. Her bright blue eyes darted back and forth between the butterfly cupcakes and the gingerbread men. 'They all look so yummy I can't decide,' she said, her breath fogging up the glass.

Pierre chuckled. 'Why not 'ave both?'

'I might not be able to fit in my dinner as well,' the child said, pressing a forefinger against her lip. She thought for a moment longer, her brows furrowing with concentration.

'You can 'ave one now and take the other one for dessert, *non*?' Pierre suggested. He gave her a wink. 'It's my treat.'

Digby Pertwhistle looked at the child. 'What do you say, Clemmie?'

The girl beamed. '*Merci*, Pierre.'

'Ah, *très bien*!' Pierre clapped his hands with delight. 'You must keep practising your French while we are gone.'

Clementine glanced up at him in surprise. 'Where are you going?' she asked.

The man's smile faltered. 'Oh dear,' he sighed. 'I thought Sophie would 'ave told you the news today.'

Clementine shook her head. 'Sophie was in the sick bay with a tummy ache and she looked really sad.'

The door opened and Mrs Bottomley shuffled into the shop. Her arms were weighed down with grocery bags. 'Good afternoon, everyone,' the woman blustered, slightly out of breath. She set down her cargo and pushed up her sleeves. 'Well, Pierre, that is exciting news about the move to Paris.'

'Are you moving to Paris, Mrs Bottomley?' Clementine asked. She was surprised no one had mentioned it at school that day.

'Of course not, Clementine,' the old woman scoffed. 'What would I do there? I don't speak French and all that rich food gives me indigestion. No, the *Rousseaus* are going back to Paris.'

Clementine's eyes widened. 'Paris,' she whispered.

Pierre nodded. 'My father is not well, so we are going to 'elp run 'is business until 'e is better,' the man explained.

'But how long is that for?' Clementine asked. She tried to remember how long she'd had to stay in bed after her appendix operation.

'Probably a year or so, I should think,' the man replied.

'A year!' Clementine exclaimed. She stood frozen to the spot as the full meaning of the words settled upon her like a heavy blanket. A year was forever.

'It will pass by in the blink of an eye, *ma chérie*,' Pierre assured her. He placed a few more gingerbread men into the bag, hoping their discovery might make Clementine feel a little better during the ride home.

'Would you mind if I popped in ahead of you, Digby?' Mrs Bottomley asked. 'I've got to dash home to prepare supper. Violet's coming round for a spot of bridge later.' The old woman bustled forward without waiting for a reply. 'I'd like a sourdough loaf and two of those large cream buns.'

Pierre nodded and took up a box and a pair of tongs. 'I see you 'ave a taste for them,' he said.

'They're delicious, especially the ones with custard *and* cream,' Mrs Bottomley replied. 'I thought Violet might enjoy one too.'

Clementine felt like time had slowed down around her, though her mind was racing a million miles a minute. 'Aunt Violet says you only have to look at one of those and your bottom gets bigger,' she said hazily.

Digby chortled, then quickly smothered his laughter with a cough.

'What was that, Clementine?' the old woman demanded. 'Did you say I have a big bottom?'

Clementine shook her head, the heat rising to her cheeks. 'No, I –'

'Goodness me, Digby,' Mrs Bottomley huffed, 'I think you need to teach that child some manners.'

'I didn't mean to . . .' Clementine tried to explain but it was no use. From a young age, she seemed to have the unfortunate knack of saying or doing things that got her into trouble despite her best intentions.

Ethel Bottomley handed over the money and gathered up her grocery bags. 'Good day to you, Pierre,' she said, rushing to the door. 'And as for you, young lady, wait until I see your great-aunt this evening!'

'But I didn't say that,' Clementine mumbled. She was beginning to feel hot and prickly in her school uniform, much like the way she did when Joshua was being mean to her.

Digby Pertwhistle gave the child's shoulder a squeeze. 'It's all right, Clemmie, *I* heard what you said,' he whispered. 'Anyway, she has got a big bottom.'

'Perhaps you should call it 'er *derrière* next time,' Pierre said cheekily. 'That means "bottom" in French.'

Clementine managed a small smile, but her face clouded over as she remembered the news. 'When are you leaving?' she asked softly.

'I am afraid it 'as all come about very suddenly,' the man replied. He hated to see the girl so upset. 'We fly out at the end of the week.'

'Have you found someone to look after the shop?' Uncle Digby asked.

Pierre nodded. '*Oui*, a man called Roger. I understand 'is daughter . . .'

Clementine heard the shop door open. She turned around to see Sophie and her brother, Jules, walk in with their mother. The two girls looked at one another and, without a word, rushed into each other's arms. Needless to say, there soon wasn't a dry eye in the shop.

NEW BEGINNINGS

Clementine finished writing her name, followed by a long line of kisses. She closed the card and studied the picture on the front. It was hard to imagine life without Sophie. The two girls did everything together – school, ballet, soccer and sleepovers. But Clementine decided to be brave for Sophie, who was also upset she had to leave.

Her mother leaned over her shoulder. 'That looks lovely, sweetheart. I like the way you've written *au revoir* at the top.'

'Aunt Violet showed me how to do it,' Clementine replied. 'It means "until we meet again", and that's me and Lavender waving goodbye.'

'I'm sure Sophie and Jules will be back before you know it,' Clarissa said.

'But why do they have to go in the first place?' Clementine asked.

'You know why. Sophie's grandfather isn't well and they're going to help him,' her mother explained. 'You'd do the same if we lived far away from Uncle Digby or Aunt Violet and they were sick, wouldn't you, darling?'

Clementine thought for a moment, then nodded. Not so long ago she wouldn't have minded living a very long way from Aunt Violet, but things were different now. Her great-aunt was a lot better behaved, and Aunt Violet's beloved sphynx cat, Pharaoh, was the best of friends with Clementine's pet pig. The two were inseparable – a bit like Clementine and Sophie.

The door from the hallway swung open and Violet Appleby stormed into the kitchen carrying a tray piled with teacups, saucers and plates. She was huffing and snorting like a pony.

Clarissa hurried over to take the tray. 'What's the matter, Aunt Violet?' she asked. 'I thought you were going to stay and chat.'

The old woman hurled herself onto one of the kitchen chairs. 'Godfathers,' she muttered, 'don't ever volunteer me to take tea with the guests again. I was in grave danger in there.'

'What happened?' Clementine asked. She had a bad feeling Aunt Violet had found the fieldmouse Pharaoh had brought in from the garden last weekend. It had escaped the jaws of death and run off into the house. Clementine had tried to tell her mother and Uncle Digby but they'd both been busy at the time. She had forgotten all about it until now.

Clarissa grimaced. 'Grave danger of what?'

The old woman rolled her eyes. 'Dying of boredom with Mr and Mrs Snoresby in there.'

Clementine giggled and picked up a pink pencil.

Violet Appleby sighed and turned to inspect Clementine's drawing. 'Interesting perspective. I like it.'

'We're having a surprise farewell party for Sophie at school tomorrow afternoon too,' the child informed her. 'Me and Poppy and the twins asked Mr Smee and he said that we could. Mummy is baking a cake for it and I'm going to help.'

'Poppy, the twins and I,' Aunt Violet corrected. 'One of these days, Clementine, you'll learn to speak the Queen's English.'

Clementine wrinkled her nose and added a love heart to her drawing.

'Speaking of cakes, we'd better get started or there'll be no time for the decorations,' Clarissa said, hurrying over to the pantry. She was just returning with an armful of ingredients when the telephone rang.

Clementine hopped down from her chair and raced over to answer it. 'Good afternoon, Penberthy House Hotel, this is Clementine speaking,' she said before breaking into a grin. 'Oh, hello. Mummy's here in the kitchen. I'll get her.'

Clarissa turned from where she was measuring out the flour. 'Who is it, darling?' she asked.

Clementine placed her hand over the mouthpiece as she'd been taught to do. 'It's Drew and he said he has big news,' she said excitedly, jigging up and down on the spot.

Drew Barnsley and his son, Will, had become firm family friends with the Applebys since filming a documentary on Penberthy House. They had kept in touch with frequent visits and countless phone calls. The trouble was, the Barnsleys lived quite a distance away and it was not always easy to arrange outings, especially with the hotel becoming busier these days.

'Oh.' Lady Clarissa patted her hands on her apron and walked over. Clementine couldn't help noticing that her mother's cheeks were flushed. Clarissa took the phone from her daughter and smiled. 'Hello there,' she said into the mouthpiece, her eyes twinkling.

Clementine watched expectantly as her mother chatted away. She wondered what the news could be. Maybe Drew and Will were getting a dog. Will had been wanting one since Clementine's neighbours, the Hobbses, got their cavoodle, Cosmo.

'That's fabulous. Clementine is going to be so thrilled,' Clarissa said. There was a short pause as she turned around and lowered her voice. 'Yes, of course. I am too,' she whispered.

'The towels are out in all the rooms and I've freshened up the flowers too,' Uncle Digby announced as he skipped down the back stairs and into the kitchen.

'Shush!' Aunt Violet hissed, madly batting a hand in his direction.

'What's the matter?' he asked.

'Mummy's on the phone to Drew and he has *big* news,' Clementine said softly.

The man's eyebrows jumped up. 'Oh, I see.'

'He'd better not be telling her they're moving to Africa,' Aunt Violet muttered.

Clementine's breath caught in her throat. She couldn't bear the thought of two friends going to live overseas in the same week.

Clarissa hung up the phone and turned around to find three pairs of eyes trained on her. 'What?' she said, blinking innocently.

'Out with it,' Aunt Violet demanded.

'What's Drew's big news?' Clementine asked her mother.

Clarissa blushed. 'It seems that Drew has . . . bought a house,' she said.

Violet Appleby and Digby Pertwhistle looked at one another and smiled. Clementine's bottom lip began to tremble. 'So they *are* moving to Africa,' the child said in a wobbly voice.

Her mother laughed. 'Of course not, Clemmie. Wherever did you get that idea?'

'Then where are they going?' Clementine asked.

Clarissa's eyes lit up and a coy smile played on her lips. 'They've bought –'

'Crabtree Cottage!' Uncle Digby and Aunt Violet chimed in unison.

Clarissa nodded, a look of complete bemusement on her face.

'Told you so,' Aunt Violet said to the old man.

'I knew first,' Uncle Digby retorted.

Clementine wondered why all the grown-ups were acting so strangely. 'Where's that?' she asked.

'Just around the corner from Mrs Mogg's shop,' Clarissa said.

Clementine's face split into a smile. 'Drew and Will are moving here? To Penberthy Floss?'

All three adults nodded.

'Hooray!' Clementine exclaimed. A starburst of happiness exploded in her heart and she scooped Lavender into her arms and danced around the kitchen. 'This week feels like being on a roller-coaster, Mummy, with all the ups and downs.'

Clarissa smiled at her daughter. 'I'm sure that it does, sweetheart. Life's like that a lot of the time – the only thing to do is strap yourself in and enjoy the ride.'

AU REVOIR

Angus ran to the door as soon as Poppy and Sophie left the room. Once he saw they had headed across the quadrangle, he turned back and shouted, 'All clear!'

The children flew into action. Teddy raced to the storeroom to fetch the balloons and bunting. Mr Smee climbed up on a chair, armed with thumbtacks and sticky tape, while Astrid and Tilda took to the whiteboard. Tilda began drawing huge colourful flowers around the edges while Astrid added all the French words she knew in the spots between.

Meanwhile, Angus and Joshua were in charge of moving the furniture. They zoomed around the room, stacking the chairs and pushing desks together to form one large table in the centre. The rest of the class then set about preparing the food. There were croissants and eclairs, macarons in blue, white and red, and even fizzy drink too. Mr Smee wouldn't usually have approved but today was a very special occasion.

Clementine proudly unveiled the marble cake she and her mother had made. It had mint-green icing and written across the top in pink were the words '*Au revoir*, Sophie' enveloped inside a huge love heart.

'Hurry up!' Teddy called from his position as lookout. 'I hear footsteps!'

'Everyone, hide!' Mr Smee whispered. 'Teddy, you can turn off the lights.'

Evie and Ally squealed with excitement. The children dived under desks while some hid in the storeroom. Joshua crouched behind Mr Smee's reading chair. The door opened and Teddy flipped on the light switch.

'Surprise!' the children screamed. They leapt out cheering and clapping.

Ethel Bottomley almost sprang out of her sturdy brown shoes. 'What on earth?' she gasped, clutching at her chest.

The children groaned.

'False alarm, it's just Mrs Bottomley,' Joshua said with disappointment.

The Kindergarten teacher spied the table of pastries and fizzy drinks and tutted loudly. 'What's going on in here?' she demanded.

'We're having a surprise farewell party for Sophie, and she and Poppy are going to be back any second,' Clementine explained. She hoped Mrs Bottomley would hurry up and leave before she spoiled everything.

'They're coming!' Teddy yelled. 'I can see them.'

'Quick, everyone, back in position,' Mr Smee whispered. He grabbed hold of Mrs Bottomley's

arm and shoved the woman into the storeroom with one swift movement. 'Just stand in there and pipe down,' he commanded.

Several children who had already hidden in the storeroom rushed out, leaving the Kindergarten teacher on her own.

Clementine smothered a laugh. She loved that Mr Smee wasn't afraid of Mrs Bottomley like all the other teachers at the school were.

The old woman's muffled voice could be heard from the other side of the door. 'But I came to talk about Grandparents' Day,' she protested. 'It's on next Friday and we still have to choose the host –'

'Nan, be quiet,' Angus hissed through the door.

Ethel began to scold the young man when an almighty shushing from the whole class finally put a stop to her jabbering. There were a few nervous giggles as the children lay in wait.

Poppy's voice carried into the room as she pushed open the door.

'Why's the room all dark?' Sophie said.

'SURPRISE!' the children yelled, leaping out from all over the place. Poor Sophie jumped into the air almost as high as Mrs Bottomley had. Teddy switched the lights back on.

'Is this for me?' Sophie said, her face crumpling.

'You didn't think we would let you leave without having a proper farewell party, did you?' Mr Smee smiled at the girl. 'It's just a small one because it won't be long at all until you're back again.'

There was a pounding on the storeroom door, and Joshua Tribble ran over to open it. Sophie was surprised to see Mrs Bottomley spill out into the room. The woman's hair was sticking up all over the place and her brown dress was as crinkled as her frown.

'Clearly now is not the right time to discuss Grandparents' Day,' Mrs Bottomley said, regaining her composure. 'Enjoy your time away, Sophie, and make sure to savour everything France has to offer.'

'Like frogs' legs and snails,' Joshua called out.

The old woman shook her head and waddled out of the room.

Mr Smee motioned for the children to gather around. 'Clementine would like to say something,' he announced.

Clementine stood up in front of the whiteboard and took a deep breath. 'I wrote a poem for Sophie.'

Joshua Tribble groaned. 'Poems are boring.'

Angus glared at the boy. 'No, they're not, and Clemmie is really good at them.'

'You're just saying that because she's your *girlfriend*,' Joshua sputtered.

Roderick Smee shot the boy a warning look. Joshua hunkered down and crossed his arms, glowering.

Clementine pulled a page from her pocket and cleared her throat. She took another deep breath and began:

When the moon rises and the stars
*   shimmer in the sky,*
I'll look up to the heavens and choose
*   the first one that I see.*

I'll call it Sophie and it will blink at
me and twinkle as if it's waving.
And when you look into the dark
night sky,
that first star you see is me,
waving right back.

Au revoir, *Sophie!*

A tear wobbled down Sophie's cheek. 'Thank you,' she whispered.

Clementine folded the piece of paper and placed it back into her pocket. 'Do you promise to come back?' she asked.

Sophie nodded. 'Do you promise to write and tell me all the news?'

'Of course,' Clementine said.

The two best friends hugged each other tightly as the rest of the class clapped and cheered.

'Three cheers for Sophie,' Angus shouted. 'Hip hip!'

'Hooray!'

MR BAKER

Clarissa Appleby snipped another long-stemmed rose and placed it in the wicker basket at her feet. She looked up to see Clementine half-heartedly nudging her soccer ball across the back lawn with Lavender trotting along beside her. She hated to see her daughter in such low spirits.

'I have to go to the butcher's in a little while, Clemmie. Would you like to come?' Clarissa called. 'We could get a gingerbread man from Pierre's?'

Clementine shook her head without looking up. 'No, thank you,' she replied.

'Uncle Digby said he met the new baker,' Clarissa added. 'Apparently, he has a little girl the same age as you. It might be nice to introduce yourself.'

Clementine shrugged and prodded the soccer ball with her foot. 'I don't want any new friends.'

'Clemmie,' her mother admonished. 'That's not like you, darling. You can never have too many friends. It's not as if this little girl will be replacing Sophie.'

Clementine's shoulders slumped as she watched the ball roll away under a bush.

Lady Clarissa put down her garden clippers and walked over to the child. She knelt in front of Clementine and, taking up both of her hands, looked into the girl's watery blue eyes. 'The good news is, Will and Drew are coming tomorrow.'

'They are?' Clementine brushed her eyes with the back of her hand.

Clarissa nodded. 'They're moving into the cottage at the end of next week but they'll come to stay with us tomorrow so that Will can start school on Monday. I'm going to have a welcome dinner for them tomorrow night and I thought we could invite the new baker and his family,' she said gently. 'Why don't you come inside and give me a hand, sweetheart?'

Clementine nodded, then scurried across the lawn to retrieve her ball. She'd never felt so mixed up inside. She was happy about Drew and Will coming, but it still didn't seem fair that Sophie had to go away for a whole year. She wondered if being really sad was like a gloomy day when, no matter how hard the sun tried, it just couldn't get through the clouds. Clementine booted the ball hard to the other end of the garden. It whistled past Aunt Violet's ear as the woman walked out the back door.

'Good heavens, that missed me by a whisker!' Violet Appleby exclaimed. 'You know, Clementine, being in a sulk is not going to make Sophie come back any sooner.'

'I'm not in a sulk,' Clementine mumbled. She took Lavender up in her arms and nuzzled the little pig.

Aunt Violet raised an eyebrow. 'Is that so? Then get your cardigan, Clemmie. You're coming with me to Highton Mill.'

Clementine pouted. 'But I don't want to.'

'I'll go,' Clarissa offered.

'No, dear,' Aunt Violet said. 'I'll drop by the butcher's and then I'll get the bread rolls you were after for tonight.'

'If you really don't mind, that would save me some time,' Clarissa replied. 'We've got a few people arriving this afternoon and I should help Uncle Digby with the beds.'

Aunt Violet nodded. 'That's settled then. Lavender can come too.'

'But you don't like her going in your car,' Clementine said.

The old woman softened. 'It's all right. Just get her lead and make sure she goes to the toilet before we leave.'

Clementine sighed and, clutching the little

pig tighter, trudged across the lawn and up the
back steps.

Violet Appleby opened the rear passenger
door. Lavender jumped down onto the path
and waited for her mistress to clamber out
after her.

'Where are we going first?' Clementine
asked, holding Lavender's red lead.

'Pierre's, to pick up the bread order,' Aunt
Violet said.

Clementine looked down the street. People
were walking in and out of the patisserie as
though nothing had changed. But everything
had. For a start, Pierre wouldn't be there. She
took a deep breath and tried again to push the
sad thoughts away.

When the three of them walked inside,
a man with a thick head of curly black hair
looked up over the top of the counter. He had
a long moustache that twirled on the ends and

wore a bold yellow apron over a purple shirt with paisley swirls. Clementine stared at the apron, wondering what had happened to Pierre's red one. She slipped her hand into her great-aunt's.

'Hello,' Aunt Violet said to the man, eyeing his attire. 'It's lovely to meet you Mr . . . Oh dear, I have only heard Digby refer to you as Roger. How ghastly of me not to know your surname. I'm Violet Appleby and this is my great-niece, Clementine Rose.'

'That's all right, Vi. We don't stand on ceremony around here,' the man said cheerfully. 'For the record, it's Baker.'

The old woman blanched. At a pinch she might have tolerated this stranger calling her by her first name, but an abbreviation was completely unacceptable. 'You can call me *Miss* Appleby,' she instructed.

Clementine giggled. 'Mr Baker is a baker,' she whispered to Lavender.

Roger Baker grinned and peered down at the pig. 'What sort of dog is that?' he asked.

Clementine laughed. 'Her name is Lavender and she's a teacup pig.'

Lavender squealed at the mention of her name.

'I've never seen such a charming little thing. Is she a baby?' the man asked.

Clementine shook her head. 'No, she's a grown-up.'

Roger Baker walked around the counter to give the tiny pig a pat. Lavender sniffed his fingers, then gave them a nibble. 'Wait until my Saskia sees her,' he said. 'She'll be insisting I get her one right away.'

'Mr Baker, I've been asked by my niece, Clarissa, to invite you and your family over to dinner with us tomorrow night at Penberthy House,' Aunt Violet said.

The man smiled and stood up. 'Oh, that would be lovely. I'll bring something for dessert.'

'We wouldn't dream of it,' Aunt Violet said. 'Come by around five and we'll start with some drinks on the terrace.'

'Wonderful,' Mr Baker said. He walked back to the other side of the counter and quickly washed his hands before passing Aunt Violet a large basket of bread rolls. 'My Sassy is going to go nuts over that pig. Lock her up, Clementine,' he warned, 'or she might just disappear home with us.'

Clementine's eyes widened in horror and she squeezed her great-aunt's hand in a vice-like grip.

Aunt Violet frowned at the man. 'Come along, Clemmie, we need to get to the butcher's before it closes. Oh, I almost forgot – what would you like?'

The child peered into the glass cabinet. For some reason the butterfly cupcakes didn't look quite so fluffy and the buttons on the gingerbread men seemed a bit skew-whiff. Clementine shook her head. 'I'm not hungry,' she said softly.

'Funny about that, me either.' Aunt Violet smiled tightly at the man. 'We'll see you tomorrow night then, Mr Baker.'

Roger gave them a friendly wave. 'Looking forward to it, Vi.'

Clementine followed Aunt Violet out onto the High Street. As the old woman launched into a speech about the decline of manners in the world today, Clementine glanced back at Pierre's patisserie. She hadn't thought it possible, but she now missed Sophie and the Rousseaus more than ever.

LOVE IS IN THE AIR

Clementine awoke early on Sunday morning. She'd had a wonderful dream, where she'd visited Sophie in Paris. The two of them had eaten croissants, drunk hot chocolate and walked along a riverbank. It had seemed so real that Clementine was met with a pang of disappointment when she opened her eyes. She lay in bed for a while and thought about what Sophie was doing that very moment.

Knowing that her mother and Uncle Digby would already be up preparing breakfast for the ten guests who had stayed overnight, Clementine quickly got dressed. She tiptoed out of her room, careful not to rouse Lavender, who was snoring gently. Clementine padded down the main stairs and stopped in front of the portraits of her grandparents.

'Hello Granny and Grandpa,' she whispered. 'Guess what? Will and Drew are coming today – and not just for a visit. They're moving to the village, which means I can see them *all* the time. Oh, and I had a dream about Sophie last night. Do you think she was dreaming about me as well?'

Digby Pertwhistle walked out of the dining room with a feather duster and a cloth in his hands. He thought he'd heard a voice and glanced up at the child. 'Good morning, Clemmie,' he said. 'Are you catching your grandparents up on recent events?'

Clementine nodded. 'I was just telling them about Drew and Will. I already told

them about Sophie. I think Granny was as upset as me.'

The old man smiled. He may have just been the butler of Penberthy House to the outside world, but he cared for the child as if she were his own granddaughter. He wondered if Clementine would soon reach a time when she stopped talking to the paintings on the wall. He hoped not. 'You'll have to write to Sophie next week and tell her all your news,' he suggested.

'I'm going to,' Clementine said. 'We made a pinky promise to write to each other every week. She's going to help me with my French and I'm going to tell her everything that's happening here so that when she gets back it won't feel like she's been away at all.'

'That sounds like the perfect plan,' the old man said, his eyes sparkling. 'Now, how would you like to have some crepes with sugar and lemon for breakfast?'

Clementine grinned. 'Yes, please! Then we can pretend we're in Paris with Sophie.'

'Quick, let's sneak some in before the guests are up,' Uncle Digby whispered, twirling the feather duster and pointing it towards the kitchen.

'Yum! Bye Granny, bye Grandpa,' Clementine called, waving to them. 'See you later.'

She then skittered down the stairs and followed Uncle Digby into the kitchen.

By midday all of the guests had left and Clementine was now helping her mother to make the chocolate mousse for tonight's dessert. It was one of Clementine's absolute favourites, especially when she got to lick the beaters. Clarissa flicked the switch on the mixer, sending it into a whirring frenzy.

'They're here!' Clementine gasped, startling her mother. The child leapt off the stool she was standing on and raced out of the kitchen, leaving the door swinging wildly in her wake. Clementine rounded the corner at full speed and bumped right into Aunt Violet, who was carrying a tray of crystal glasses. The woman spun around on the spot. Clementine held her breath as the glasses wobbled dangerously. One teetered on the edge and the child reached out just in time to catch it.

'Clementine! Slow down, for heaven's sake,' the old woman scolded. 'This crystal is *irreplaceable*. It belonged to your great-great-grandparents.'

Clementine winced. 'I'm sorry, Aunt Violet, but Drew and Will are here!' The child quickly returned the glass to the tray and skidded across the entrance foyer to the front door.

'Well, why didn't you say so before?' Aunt Violet placed the tray onto the side table by the stairs. She smoothed her hair and checked her reflection in the mirror. 'Hurry up and open the door, Clementine.'

The child, who had been waiting impatiently, gladly grabbed the handle and pulled hard. Will and Drew were standing on the porch smiling.

'Hello!' Clementine shouted, her excitement bubbling over.

'Good afternoon, gorgeous girl,' Drew said, giving her a great big hug.

Clementine giggled and rubbed her cheek. 'You've got prickles.'

'I do?' Drew smiled. 'Sorry about that. I couldn't find my razor this morning. I must have packed it into one of the hundreds of boxes by mistake.'

'Welcome to Penberthy Floss,' Aunt Violet said, unable to wipe the silly grin off her face. 'I hear the village has some new residents.'

Drew smiled. 'Thank you. It's wonderful to be here.'

'Do you want to build a cubby?' Clementine asked Will. 'Lavender and I have been waiting for you all day. I thought we could make up a play and Mummy said we can use the video camera.'

The boy looked at his father.

'Go on,' Drew said, giving him a reassuring pat on the shoulder.

Will smiled and nodded, and the two children were soon galloping away down the hall.

Clementine opened the library door. 'This is the best spot for cubbies,' she explained.

'It's so big,' Will agreed. 'We'll be able to build a whole city of cubbies.'

'Are you happy you're moving to Penberthy Floss?' Clementine asked. 'My friend Sophie just moved to France and I miss her a lot.'

Will nodded. 'I'll miss my old friends too but I can visit them. You should see my new bedroom. It's got the whole universe painted on the ceiling and there are even stars that twinkle. They're really lights but they look like stars. Dad says we can get a dog soon.'

'What will you call it?' Clementine asked.

Will shrugged. 'You can help me think of some names.'

'Oops, I forgot that we need some sheets for the cubby,' Clementine said. 'I have to ask Mummy which ones we can use.'

The pair charged back down the hall and around the corner, but an unfamiliar sight stopped them in their tracks. They peered into the entrance hall at the silhouette of two figures. Will looked at Clementine. 'Are they . . .?'

Clementine tilted her head and nodded. 'I think so.'

Drew released Clarissa, whose face was a darker shade of pink than the long-stemmed roses on the hall table.

Clementine and Will ran towards them. 'Are you in love?' Clementine asked.

Drew and Clarissa looked at the children and then at each other. Clarissa had been meaning to speak to Clementine all week but, with Sophie leaving, she'd thought the poor child had enough changes to deal with. Clarissa's heart thumped. 'Clemmie, I was going to talk to you,' she began.

'Why?' Clementine asked.

'Well, I should have said something before now,' her mother explained.

Clementine frowned. 'Mummy, Drew's loved you ever since the filming. Didn't you

know? Can we please get some sheets for our cubby?'

Drew and Clarissa looked at one another and laughed. 'Are you okay, buddy?' Drew asked his son.

'Of course,' Will said. 'I knew that's why you wanted to move here. I heard you on the phone lots of times all lovey-dovey.'

Clementine giggled.

'Now I get to play with Clemmie all the time,' Will added. 'We're making the biggest cubby ever, and Clemmie's going to help me think of a name for our new dog.'

'Mummy, can we get the sheets now?' Clementine asked. 'We want to get started straight away.'

Clarissa smiled at Drew as he wrapped his arm around her waist. 'Absolutely,' she said. 'Let's see what this cubby is going to look like, shall we?'

FRIENDS AND FOES

Clementine and Will's cubby covered almost the entire library. Lavender and Pharaoh had spent part of the afternoon playing chasings in and out of the sheets until the pair of them had fallen sound asleep under one of the armchairs. Clementine was shooting a close-up of Lavender while Will narrated in a deep and frothy voice, like a man he had heard on the television.

'We've just stumbled upon a rather unusual hog. I'm not sure of the species but perhaps it's teacupis piggis,' the boy said.

'Clemmie! Will!' Clarissa called. 'You'd better get changed. The Bakers will be arriving soon.' The woman walked into the room, wondering where the children were.

Clementine crawled out from under the covers and stood up. 'Can we leave the cubby here?' she begged with pleading eyes.

'Why not? We don't have any guests in until mid-next week,' her mother replied. 'Just don't tell Aunt Violet.'

'Don't tell Aunt Violet what?' the old woman asked, appearing behind her niece. She was wearing a silk blouse and striking teal green skirt, which Clementine thought looked lovely on her. 'Godfathers! What's all this mess?'

'Will and I made a cubby in the jungle,' Clementine informed her. She pointed behind the woman and gasped. 'Watch out for the hippo, Aunt Violet! They look cute but they're really fierce.'

Violet Appleby flicked her hand and stood tall. 'Hippo schmippo! That beast wouldn't stand a chance against me. Now, hurry up and pack this away,' she instructed.

'But Mummy said we can leave it up and play here tomorrow after school,' Clementine protested.

Aunt Violet fiddled with the pearls around her neck. 'Well, you'd better lock the door. I don't want that Mr Baker telling people the place is a mess.'

'Why? What was he like?' Clarissa asked. She'd been so busy that she hadn't had a chance to ask about him.

'Put it this way, Clarissa. He's no Pierre,' said Violet Appleby.

Clementine remembered what Mr Baker had said about taking Lavender. She looked over at the armchair the little pig was underneath, still sound asleep, and felt a pang of worry. 'Aunt Violet, should we hide Lavender?'

'Why on earth would you need to hide her?' Lady Clarissa asked. She was now intrigued to know what had happened during their visit to the patisserie.

'I'm sure Mr Baker was just joking, Clementine,' Aunt Violet said, quickly explaining the situation to Clarissa. 'But perhaps we should leave them in here to be on the safe side.'

The children left their video camera and the pets and followed Lady Clarissa out of the room. Aunt Violet locked the door and put the key into her pocket.

Clementine and Will had just begun a game of Snakes and Ladders when the doorbell rang.

'They're late,' Aunt Violet said tersely as she fished around in the drawer for a pair of salad servers. 'I told them to be here at five.'

Clementine rolled the die and glanced at the clock. The big hand was on the three, which meant it was quarter past the hour. Digby Pertwhistle was already on the terrace by the billiard room, firing up the barbecue. As there were currently no guests in the hotel, he had opted out of formal attire and had donned beige trousers and a short-sleeved blue shirt.

Lady Clarissa placed the last strawberry on top of the huge bowl of chocolate mousse. 'Do you want to come with me, Clemmie?' she asked. 'I'm going to take the Bakers straight to the terrace.'

'Okay,' Clementine replied, sliding off her chair. She wondered if Mr Baker's daughter would like any of the same things she did, like ballet and poems.

'I'll start on the drinks,' Drew said. He'd already helped Digby to set up a makeshift bar and had come back inside to collect the ice buckets.

Will scooped the board and pieces into its box. 'I'll come with you, Dad.'

Father and son headed out of the kitchen and around the rear hall to the billiard room, which had recently been renovated. It had been shut off for years, the receptacle of more junk than Clarissa cared to remember. But in the past few months the billiard table had been unearthed, the walls repapered and the cobwebs done away with. It was proving to be a huge hit with the guests and had direct access to a lovely terrace, which could now be put to proper use. Clarissa wished she had reinstated it years ago but, with a total of sixty rooms, there was always too much to do at Penberthy House.

The bell rang again just as Clarissa opened the door. A woman with a mane of platinum-blonde curls that reached almost to her waist stood beside Roger Baker. She wore towering red heels, which bumped her up a couple of inches taller than her husband, and her red dress clung to her every curve. The child in front of them looked like a miniature version of Mrs Baker with equally long hair. She was wearing a black skirt, a silver sequinned midriff top and a pout to match.

'Hello, welcome to Penberthy House,' Clarissa said with a smile.

'Sorry, Roger didn't say whether we were supposed to dress up or not,' the woman said, giving Clarissa's sundress and cardigan the once-over.

Clarissa was about to answer when Mr Baker jumped in. 'You must be Clarissa Appleby. I'm Roger and this is my wife, Chanelle, and my daughter, Saskia.' He turned to his wife and daughter. 'And this is Clemmie Rose. I told you she was a little cutie.'

'Where's your pig?' his daughter demanded. 'Daddy said you've got a pig and I want to see it.'

Clementine gulped and looked at the man.

'Sassy, I'm sure that Clemmie Rose will show you the pig soon,' her mother cooed, 'although I can't imagine for the life of me why you'd want a pig as a pet. They're so dirty and smelly.'

'Lavender is actually very clean,' Clementine said. 'She's lovely but she's asleep at the moment.'

Saskia stamped her foot. 'But Daddy said that I could see her.'

'Perhaps you can later,' Clarissa said, smiling at the girl. 'Now, why don't we go through to the terrace? I believe Uncle Digby's got the barbecue started.'

Mrs Baker's head swivelled from side to side as the group piled into the entrance foyer. 'What a beautiful house,' she gushed. 'Look at those portraits.'

'That's Granny and Grandpa,' Clementine said. 'I told them you were coming tonight.'

Saskia curled her top lip. 'They're not *real* people.'

'I know,' Clementine replied, shrinking into her mother's side, 'but I like to think they're still here and part of the family.'

'That's so stupid,' Saskia muttered under her breath.

Lady Clarissa put an arm around her daughter. 'Please follow me,' she said, leading the way to the billiard room. The group exited through the French doors and onto the patio, where the barbecue was sizzling away. As if on cue, Drew popped a champagne cork.

'Ooh, who do we have here?' Mrs Baker simpered.

Drew set down the bottle and held out his hand. 'Hello, I'm Drew and this is my son, Will,' he said, nodding towards the boy, who was standing beside him.

'It's a pleasure to meet you both. I'm Chanelle and this is Sassy and my husband, Roger,' the woman said.

Uncle Digby turned from the grill and shook hands with Mr Baker. 'Hello again,' he said warmly.

Saskia pointed at Aunt Violet, who had just appeared in the doorway. 'Is that your wife?' she asked.

'Godfathers no!' the old woman sputtered. 'Just because we're a similar vintage doesn't mean we're married. Mr Pertwhistle is our *butler*.'

Chanelle's heavily made-up face creased with confusion. 'How curious. I thought butlers wore those funny penguin suits and didn't speak unless they were spoken to.'

'I'm glad to say we don't observe such rules here,' Clarissa said, shooting Aunt Violet a glare. 'Uncle Digby began working for my father a long time ago and has become a very dear member of our family. I honestly don't know how we would cope without him.'

The old man winked at her in gratitude and turned back to tend the barbecue.

'Do you want to play a game?' Clementine asked Saskia. 'We have Snakes and Ladders.'

Saskia rolled her eyes. 'I hate that one.'

'I've got a soccer ball?' Clementine offered hopefully.

'I *hate* soccer too,' Saskia spat. 'I want to see the pig!'

Clementine and Will looked at one another. 'But Lavender's asleep,' Clementine said.

'That's not fair. Daddy said,' Saskia whined.

'I've got an idea. Why don't we make a movie instead?' Will suggested.

Saskia flicked her hair over her shoulders. 'Only if I can be the star.'

'I'll go and get the camera,' Will said, heading over to Aunt Violet to ask her for the library key.

Clementine looked across at her mother, who winked. Not that they knew it, but both of them were already thinking it was going to be a long night ahead.

SPOILED ROTTEN

R oger Baker wandered over to talk to Uncle Digby. They were soon comparing barbecuing techniques while Drew pulled out some chairs for the rest of the party. Clarissa thought Chanelle might be keen to know about the children's school or some of the community activities she could become involved with, but it seemed that the woman's top priority was to locate a hairdresser and beautician. Clarissa gave her a few suggestions, although having her nails done was not something she'd ever fussed about and she couldn't remember the last time she'd had a facial. Aunt Violet was a little more helpful but Drew just nodded and smiled politely. He didn't have the foggiest idea about paraffin pedis or mini-waxes. It all sounded rather painful as far as he was concerned.

Clementine scratched around for something to say to Saskia while they waited for Will to return. She tried to take extra care with her words as the girl seemed to bite at every syllable she uttered. 'Would you like a drink?' she finally asked. 'We have some home-made lemonade.'

Saskia shrugged. Clementine carefully poured two glasses and another for Will, which she left on the tray. She passed Saskia hers.

The girl peered into the cloudy liquid. 'What's that stuff?' she asked, pointing into the glass.

'It's just the little bits of lemon,' Clementine replied. 'There's ice in there too.'

Saskia sniffed the glass suspiciously and pulled a face. 'It doesn't smell like lemonade.'

'It tastes yummy,' Clementine assured her. 'Mummy taught me how to make it and all the guests love it in summertime.'

Saskia lifted the glass to her lips and took the smallest of sips, then spat it out all over the place. 'That's disgusting!' the girl declared.

Clementine frowned and sniffed her glass, then took a tentative sip. It tasted perfectly all right to her.

'MUMMY!' Saskia screeched at the top of her lungs. 'Clemmie Rose said this was lemonade and it doesn't even have any fizz and it's got bits in it.' The girl tipped the rest of the contents onto the terrace.

'Sassy!' Roger reprimanded. 'Stop that now!'

Saskia spun around and glared at her father. 'You can't tell me what to do!' she shouted, throwing her glass onto the sandstone pavers. Everyone watched on in dismay as it smashed into a thousand tiny pieces.

Clementine gasped.

Aunt Violet's mouth flapped open as she stared at the child. 'Good heavens, what do you think you're doing?'

A low groan quickly escalated to a high-pitched wail. Uncle Digby covered his ears as Roger Baker stalked over to the girl. He grabbed her by the arms, which were now flailing about like washing on the line in a fierce wind.

'Don't tell me what to do,' Saskia roared.

Mrs Baker turned to Drew in desperation. 'Quickly, do you have some proper lemonade?' she asked.

Drew didn't miss a beat. He jumped out of his seat and pulled a bottle from the bucket of ice nearby.

Chanelle snatched it from his hand and tottered over to her daughter. 'Sassy, darling, Mummy's got you some real lemonade. You don't have to drink that nasty home-made brew.'

Saskia continued warbling for a few seconds before she stopped and took the glass from her mother. She raised it to her lips and gulped it down.

Chanelle pushed a stray curl away from the girl's face. 'Is that better, honey bunch?'

Saskia nodded. She blinked her big amber eyes and fat tears rolled down her cheeks.

'Oh, Sassy, don't cry. Daddy didn't mean to be angry,' Mrs Baker said, stroking her daughter's hair.

Violet Appleby shook her head and tutted. 'Surely Mrs Baker is not rewarding that dreadful behav–'

Clarissa scraped back her chair. 'Aunt Violet, could you give me a hand in the kitchen?' she asked.

The old woman rolled her eyes and stood up. 'I'd have had the child standing on one leg in the middle of the back lawn for the rest of the evening,' she hissed.

'She's a high-spirited little thing, isn't she?' Clarissa said, wishing Aunt Violet would keep her voice down.

Violet Appleby threw her niece a look. 'Clementine is high-spirited at times, Clarissa,' she said pointedly. '*That* child, however, is a downright menace to society.'

The two women entered the billiard room and passed Will, who was heading in the opposite direction. The boy had been struggling with the lock on the library door and had missed the commotion.

'What happened?' he asked, surveying the mess.

'Just a little accident,' Chanelle said.

'Is that what we're going to call it?' Uncle Digby muttered under his breath as he swept up the glass.

'Well, kids, why don't you go off and make a movie?' Roger said. 'Sassy, be sure that everyone gets a turn in front of the camera.'

Saskia's lip dropped and Clementine braced herself for another tantrum. 'Come on, let's go,' the child said, eager to avoid a repeat performance of the girl's earlier behaviour. 'I know a tree we can climb.'

'But I don't climb trees,' Saskia protested.

Clementine sighed. She was beginning to wonder if there was anything in the world the girl actually did like to do.

FAMILY MATTERS

Saskia followed Clementine and Will across the back lawn. 'What are we going to do for the movie?' she asked.

'We could make up a story,' Clementine suggested. 'What if we turn into pirates? The oak tree over there can be our ship.'

'I don't want to be a pirate,' Saskia said, kicking a tuft of grass. '*I* want to be a princess and *you* have to be an evil witch and then *he* has to save me.' She pointed at Will.

Clementine smiled. 'Okay. What about if, in the end, the evil witch turns out to be good?' she said.

'No, that's stupid. Everyone knows the witch is *always* evil and the princess *always* has to be rescued,' Saskia snapped.

'Princesses can look after themselves, you know,' Clementine said. 'They don't *always* have to be anything.'

Saskia scoffed. She bent down to pick up a stick and broke it into little bits. 'Does your mum love his dad?' she asked after a while.

Clementine nodded.

Saskia pulled a face like she had stepped in dogs' droppings. 'Gross.'

'No, it's not,' Will said.

'They'll probably get married and have a baby and then they won't care about you two anymore,' Saskia said, smirking. 'That's what happened to my cousin. Her dad got married to this horrible lady and they had a baby and now they ignore her and she has to sleep in a cupboard.'

'That wouldn't happen to us,' Clementine said. 'That's not even true.'

'Yes, it is. You don't know anything about my cousin,' Saskia retorted, folding her arms across her chest. 'Where's your dad, anyway?'

Clementine shrugged. She wished it was dinnertime already.

'She was adopted,' Will said, to Clementine's dismay.

'Then it will be even worse because *she's* not your real mother,' Saskia said.

Clementine felt her tummy twist.

Saskia turned her attention to Will. 'Where's your mum?'

Clementine waited for him to reply but the boy said nothing. 'She died,' Clementine said. Will looked at her with angry eyes. 'Well, she did,' the child said, her stomach clenching again. She wondered if she was having another appendicitis. The doctor had said that you only had one appendix and he'd taken that out, but maybe Clementine had two and he'd missed the second one.

'You didn't have to tell her that,' Will whispered.

'And you didn't have to tell her I was adopted,' Clementine replied. She didn't know why she was so angry. She had never worried about telling people that Uncle Digby and Pierre had found her in a basket of dinner rolls. But Saskia was different to her other friends. Even Joshua didn't seem quite so bad at the moment.

'Well, are we going to make this movie or not?' Saskia sighed.

Will's brow furrowed. 'I don't feel like it anymore.'

'Me either,' Clementine said.

'I told Mummy you'd be babies,' Saskia said, rolling her eyes. She stalked back across the lawn and around to the terrace, leaving the two friends on their own.

'Do you think what she said is true?' Clementine asked.

Will shook his head. 'No, my dad would never marry your mum.'

Clementine suddenly felt very cross. 'Good. I don't want them to get married anyway.' She spun around and stomped to the other end of the garden. Will turned and skulked off in the opposite direction.

Lady Clarissa watched as Clementine pushed a potato around her plate. Her daughter had unexpectedly insisted on sitting beside her at the dinner table, while Will sat next to his father at the opposite end of the table. She was surprised the children hadn't wanted to sit together and had a feeling their young guest might have had a part to play in the matter.

'Eat your dinner, darling,' Clarissa whispered.

'I'm not hungry,' Clementine replied. She felt awful, as if she had swallowed a whole loaf of bread and it was now stuck in her throat.

'So, Drew, what do you do for a living?' Roger asked. His moustache danced about as he chewed on a sausage.

'I'm a cameraman and sound technician,' Drew replied.

Roger looked at him in surprise. 'I can't imagine there'd be much call for that sort of thing around here,' he said.

'I work all over the place,' Drew explained. 'That's how I came to know the Applebys. A colleague of mine, Basil Hobbs, happens to be their neighbour. He recently made a documentary about Penberthy House and I worked on the production.'

'Ooh, how interesting. Has it been on telly yet?' Chanelle asked.

'No, it's on next month. I think Basil's going to host a screening for everyone here in the village first,' Drew said. 'Clemmie's the star of the whole thing.'

Clementine looked up at the mention of her name.

Saskia glared across the table at her. '*She* is going to be on TV?'

'Yes,' Aunt Violet said proudly. 'Clementine did the most wonderful job playing the roles

10

of the women who have lived in the house, including myself. She's also going to be the host of Grandparents' Day at school next week.'

Clementine frowned and felt another stabbing pain in her side. 'I don't know for sure yet, Aunt Violet,' she whispered.

'*I* should be on TV,' Saskia said. 'I'm much prettier.'

'Sassy,' her father chided. 'Clemmie Rose is lovely.'

'But I'm lovelier,' the child insisted.

'Right, has everyone finished?' Lady Clarissa said, taking the opportunity to change the topic. She stood up and began to clear the plates. 'I've got chocolate mousse for dessert. That should sweeten things up.'

'I wouldn't bet on it,' Aunt Violet muttered into her napkin as she dabbed at the corners of her mouth.

'I'll help you with those.' Drew stood up and took the pile of dirty dishes from Clarissa.

Chanelle frowned and looked over at Uncle Digby. 'Isn't that *your* job?'

'He's not on duty,' Aunt Violet quipped, quick to leap to the man's defence this time. 'But I'll come and help if you like, Clarissa.'

'It's all right. We won't be a minute.' The woman smiled at Uncle Digby, who gave her a wink. They'd never seen Aunt Violet so keen to be helpful.

Clementine slipped down from her seat.

'And where are you off to?' Aunt Violet asked the girl.

'Please may I be excused? I need to go to the toilet,' Clementine said quietly, her voice almost a whisper. With a nod from her great-aunt, she padded inside.

Clementine didn't really need to go to the toilet, though her tummy did feel all mixed up. She couldn't help worrying that what Saskia had said was true. If her mother and Drew did get married and have a baby, it would be their very own. What if they liked the baby better than her? Would they send her away? They couldn't do that to Will because Drew was his real dad, but Clementine didn't even know who she really belonged to. It had never occurred to her before but Saskia seemed to know a lot about these things. Clementine reached the kitchen door and pushed it open. She gasped as she saw Drew bending down on one knee and her mother reaching out towards him.

'Mummy!' she cried, racing into the kitchen and sliding between the pair.

'What's the matter, darling?' Clarissa asked. She scooped the charging girl into her arms.

Clementine hugged the woman tightly. 'I don't feel well,' she murmured into her mother's neck.

'Oh, sweetheart, has something upset you?' Clarissa asked, stroking the girl's hair. 'Is it Saskia?'

Clementine nodded, not wanting to tell her mother what was really on her mind. She turned around to find Drew still on one knee, cleaning up a splodge of mayonnaise on the floor.

'The Bakers will be on their way after dessert and then you can tell me all about it,' Clarissa said. She set Clementine back onto the ground and fixed her ribbon. 'Do you want to help me take out the mousse?'

'Okay,' Clementine replied, eager to stay by her mother's side.

Drew looked over and flashed the child a warm smile. 'Don't worry about Saskia, Clemmie,' he said. 'She's just jealous, that's all. You're the only girl I know who has a teacup pig and is about to be a television star.'

Clementine nodded and dropped her eyes to the floor. As she followed her mother to the door, she looked up and glimpsed Drew's reflection in one of the glass doors of the sideboard. She saw him put something into his pocket and, quickly turning away, hoped it wasn't true.

A VERY BAD DAY

Clementine hardly slept a wink that night. She had stared at the ceiling for what seemed like hours on end, imagining all sorts of terrible things. When she had finally dropped off to sleep, she'd had the most awful dream. Clementine yawned and rubbed her sleepy eyes.

Roderick Smee looked over at the child. 'Were you up late last night, Clemmie?'

The girl nodded and yawned again. 'Sorry, Mr Smee, I can't seem to stop,' she sighed.

'We went to Clementine's hotel for a barbecue,' Saskia said. She was sitting beside Clementine in Sophie's old seat.

'How nice,' the man said.

Saskia made a face. 'Her mum didn't cook anything I liked to eat.'

Clementine was about to say something mean back when she remembered what her mother always told her about saying not-nice things. She closed her mouth and remained quiet.

Mr Smee wondered whether seating the new girl beside Clementine had been the right decision. He scanned Clementine's answers to the subtraction questions and smiled. 'Well, for someone who's tired, you're doing a very good job,' he said. He moved on and was surprised to find Saskia's page had barely been touched. 'Would you like some help?' he asked.

Saskia smiled sweetly. 'No, thank you. I can do it. It's just that my pencil broke and I couldn't find the sharpener.'

'This is too hard,' Joshua grumbled loudly. 'I hate subtraction. It's stupid.'

'Wait a sec, Josh – I'm coming,' the teacher said, and walked across to the other side of the room.

Saskia leaned over and hurriedly copied Clementine's answers onto her own page.

'That's cheating,' Clementine said.

Saskia plastered on a fake smile and emptied her pencil shavings all over Clementine's desk.

Clementine gasped. 'Don't do that.'

'Do what?' Saskia blew the shavings onto the floor.

'I saw you copy me,' Clementine said.

'No, you didn't,' Saskia snipped. 'I was just checking that you had the right answers.'

Clementine pulled a book out of her desk and used it to cover her work. Saskia glared at her.

There was a loud rapping at the door and Mrs Bottomley barged in. 'Good morning, Year One,' the old woman said. 'Mr Smee, I trust that everything is back to normal in here after last Friday's shenanigans.'

Clementine could hardly believe Sophie's party had only been a few days ago. So much had happened since then.

'Children, we need to talk about the arrangements for Friday,' Mrs Bottomley said. 'Now, has everyone remembered to invite their grandparents along for the special concert and classroom activities?'

All but one child nodded. Saskia put up her hand. 'I don't know what we're doing because I'm new,' she said importantly.

Mrs Bottomley looked at her. 'That's all right. Mr Smee will give you a note and hopefully you have grandparents who are not too far away.'

The child's eyes instantly began to fill with tears. 'But Fifi and Dodge died,' she blubbered.

'Who's that?' Clementine asked.

'My grandparents,' Saskia sniffed.

Mrs Bottomley clasped her hands in front of her. 'I see. Well, you can invite an elderly friend. There are lots of children doing that. Clementine is bringing her Aunt Violet and Uncle Digby.'

'But I don't know any old people,' Saskia whined.

'You can borrow my nan,' Angus said cheekily.

'I don't want your nan,' the girl snapped. 'She's probably got blue hair and wrinkles and smells funny.'

There was a ripple of giggles around the room. Mrs Bottomley's mouth opened and closed like a goldfish and Roderick Smee did all he could to stifle a laugh.

'*She's* his nan,' Joshua said with delight, pointing at Mrs Bottomley.

'You tricked me!' Saskia screeched in the most unforgiving manner, then promptly burst into tears.

Roderick Smee walked over to the girl. 'It's all right, Saskia. I'll speak with your mother this afternoon. I'm sure we can work something out.'

Ethel Bottomley offered the child a handful of tissues. 'No need to cry about it. There are plenty of other children in the same boat.'

'Yeah, my granny kicked the bucket,' Joshua said. 'Before I was even born.'

Lester nodded. 'Same.'

'Enough! Please, have some respect, boys,' Mrs Bottomley ordered. 'I want everyone in the hall straight after lunch for a full rehearsal. We have songs to practise.' The woman proceeded to read out the names of the children who were to recite stories and poems on the day. Clementine was among them. 'And remember that I still have to choose the host of the show,' Mrs Bottomley reminded them.

All of a sudden Saskia stopped her bawling. 'I could do that,' she said, perking up, 'seeing as though I don't have anyone.'

'Well, you can try out at the rehearsal,' the woman said.

Clementine stared at the girl next to her. She wanted that part and Saskia knew it.

Clementine grabbed the soccer ball as the rest of the children raced down onto the oval. 'Do you want to play?' she called out to Saskia. The girl had so far spent the whole of lunchtime complaining about the yucky fish fingers they'd had for lunch and telling the children how much better things were at her old school.

Saskia shook her head. 'I told you yesterday that I don't like soccer.'

Clementine shrugged, somewhat relieved, and jogged away with Poppy. She waved to Will, who was running around with some of the older kids in Year Two.

'She's a bit bossy,' Poppy whispered.

Clementine nodded. 'She's worse than that.'

It wasn't long before there was a giant game of soccer underway. The children raced up and down the oval shouting and cheering. After a while of sitting on her own, Saskia slunk over to the sidelines.

'Do you want to be on our team?' Joshua asked the girl.

'I suppose,' she said, and wandered onto the field.

'I thought she didn't like soccer,' Poppy said to Clementine.

Will raced along, dribbling the ball. He then booted it to Clementine, who broke free of the pack. Joshua sped across from the other side of the field. Just as Clementine was about to go for the goal, the boy raised his leg and kicked as hard as he could – right into Clementine's shin.

'Ow!' she screamed, and fell to the ground.

'Sorry,' Joshua yelled, sprinting away with the ball. He kicked it out to Saskia just before being tackled by Lester. The girl charged up the field and booted the ball straight past Evie, who was playing with her doll in the dirt, and into the back of the net.

Joshua high-fived Saskia and ran back to the middle of the field, where Clementine was still sitting on the ground holding her leg. She was trying her hardest to stop the tears from spilling. Will knelt down beside her and put an arm around her shoulder.

'Hey, Angus,' Joshua shouted, 'Clemmie's got a new boyfriend.'

Angus gave the lad a dark look. 'She's not my girlfriend!'

'Ooh,' Saskia called in a singsong voice. 'His dad is her mum's boyfriend too. He'll be her brother when they get married.' The girl smiled smugly as if she knew a secret no one else did.

'Is your mum getting married?' Poppy asked.

Clementine's face flushed. She stood up and pushed Will out of the way. 'No, she's not!' she shouted.

'Her mum loves his dad and they're going to get married and have a baby,' Saskia teased.

Joshua laughed.

'It's not true!' Clementine said, her eyes brimming with tears.

Will stalked towards the new girl. 'Stop saying that!'

'Why? What's the matter? You said so yourself they were in love,' Saskia said, feigning innocence. 'People in love get married and have babies.'

Roderick Smee noticed the small crowd of children in the middle of the oval. He walked over to see what was going on. 'Is everything

all right here?' he said, noticing Clementine's face streaked with tears.

'Clemmie got kicked in the shin by Joshua,' Tilda said.

'Do you want to get an icepack?' the man said kindly. 'Tilda can go with you.'

Clementine nodded and took the girl's hand.

'Did anything else happen?' the teacher said, glancing around at the group.

'Joshua was teasing Clemmie and Will and then Saskia joined in too,' Poppy said. She was already fed up with their new arrival.

Mr Smee scratched his head. 'I see. I hope that's not true.'

'I didn't do anything,' Saskia said in a trembling voice.

'Try to be kind to one another,' the teacher said. 'You've only got a few minutes until the bell – I suggest you get out there and have a good run around.'

Angus picked up the ball and jogged away. Roderick Smee stood on the sideline to watch over the rest of the game. Saskia had only been in his class for half a day but he already had a sneaking suspicion the girl was going to rival Joshua in the trouble stakes.

OUT OF SORTS

Clementine studied the page, then glanced up. Ethel Bottomley and the children were gathered in the assembly hall to watch the audition for the role of host. Clementine was up first. She wished she could stop thinking about what Saskia had said, but the girl's voice was stuck in her head like an annoying tune. Clementine's eyes wandered over to the girl, who shot her tongue out at her like a lizard. Clementine frowned and looked back at the page.

'We don't have all day, Clemmie,' Mrs Bottomley urged.

The girl nodded and stepped up to the microphone. 'Welcome to our Grandparents' Day celebrity,' Clementine stumbled. 'Oops, I meant celebration.'

'Thank you, Clementine, that's enough,' the teacher said. 'Joanna, you're up next.'

Clementine's cheeks burned and she felt as though she might cry. 'But I can do it better,' she said.

Mrs Bottomley looked at her watch. 'I'm afraid we don't have time.'

Joanna was jigging up and down on the spot as if she needed the toilet. At the mention of her name, she stepped forward and took the script. Eager to prove herself, the Year Two girl read the first three lines so quickly it all sounded like mumbo jumbo. Mrs Bottomley thanked her and then passed the page to Saskia, who read the entire opening without making a single mistake.

'Thank you, girls,' the teacher said. 'Given

that Clemmie already has a poem to recite and Joanna is a member of the dance group, Saskia can be the host.'

Clementine felt her eyes sting. It wasn't fair. She knew she could have done it perfectly if she hadn't been distracted by Saskia and all the mean things the girl had said at lunchtime.

'Bad luck,' Saskia whispered as they made their way to sit down. She flicked her hair back and preened.

Clementine sniffled and went to sit next to Poppy.

The rest of the afternoon dragged on. Clementine was so flustered she also fluffed the lines of her poem, which made Mrs Bottomley very cross. Saskia giggled at her and made a face when no one was looking. Clementine usually loved school but she would rather have been anywhere else that afternoon.

When the school day finally came to an end, Will joined Clementine at the gate. 'Are you okay?' he asked.

Clementine rubbed her shin and nodded. The spot where Joshua had kicked her had already swelled into a big bump.

'There's Dad,' Will said, pointing at the four-wheel drive pulling up to the kiss-and-drop area.

Lady Clarissa stepped out of the passenger seat. 'Hello there,' she called to the pair. 'Hop in.'

Clementine spotted Saskia walking past with a smirk on her face. She was with her mother, who was wearing even taller heels than the ones she'd had on the evening before.

'Hello Saskia, how was your first day?' Clarissa asked.

'I'm the host for Grandparents' Day,' the child boasted.

Clarissa smiled. 'Goodness, that's exciting,' she said. She hoped Clementine wasn't too upset at the news.

Clementine clambered into the back of Drew's car without saying goodbye. She shuffled over as Will hopped in beside her.

'We'd better run,' Mrs Baker said. 'Sassy's getting her hair coloured this afternoon. She's as brown as a fieldmouse without it. Lucky I got an appointment, seeing that she has the main part on Friday!' The woman giggled and threw them all air kisses before whisking her daughter along the street.

Drew looked at Clarissa as she climbed back into the car. 'Did Mrs Baker just say what I thought she said?'

'She certainly did,' Clarissa replied.

Drew grimaced. 'How old does she think Saskia is? I want our kids to stay kids for as long as possible.' He smiled at Clarissa and reached across to squeeze her hand.

Clementine thought back to what Saskia had said and went pale. The girl might have been right after all.

'We've got a big surprise for you two,' Drew said, glancing at the children in the rear-vision mirror. 'Are you all right, Clemmie?' he asked, noticing the expression on the girl's face.

'I've got a tummy-ache,' she lied, and leaned her head against the window.

'Oh, that's no good,' the man said. 'We were going to go for a milkshake and a treat at Pierre's.'

'It's not Pierre's anymore. It's Roger's,' Clementine huffed. 'Can we just go home?'

Drew frowned at Clarissa, who turned around and patted her daughter's leg. 'Did something happen at school today?' she asked. 'Are you sad about not being picked to host Grandparents' Day?'

'No, I just want to go home,' the child said. 'Can you help me with my homework, Mummy?'

'I can give you a hand,' Drew offered.

Clementine shook her head. 'I want Mummy to do it.'

'Okay, sweetheart,' Clarissa said. 'I guess our big surprise will have to wait.' She put away the envelope she had pulled out of her handbag.

'Don't you want to know what it is?' Drew asked.

Clementine shook her head again.

'What about you, Will?' Drew asked.

'I don't feel like any surprises at the moment,' Will mumbled.

And that was that. The children didn't say a word the entire way home, despite Drew and Clarissa's best attempts. Once Drew turned into the gravel drive, Clementine seemed to breathe a little easier.

'When are you moving into your house?' she asked Drew as the engine shut off.

'On Sunday,' Drew replied. 'The builder still has a few more things to do and I have a bit of painting to finish before then. That reminds me, Clarissa – can we have a look at that cupboard this afternoon?'

Clementine sat up straight in her seat. 'What cupboard?' she asked.

'You know the one,' her mother said. 'It was a servant's bedroom a long time ago. I don't imagine we'll need to use it as a bedroom again, so I suggested that Drew store his things in there.'

'Never say never,' Drew said with a grin.

Clementine had heard enough. She jumped out of the car and scampered through the back door. She dropped her bag on the floor and collected Lavender from her basket.

'I need to talk to you,' she said, and carried the little pig up to her bedroom. Lavender nuzzled into Clementine's neck as the child told her everything.

Lady Clarissa was perplexed. As far as she could tell, there was nothing particularly tricky about Clementine's homework and it certainly wasn't anything the girl couldn't manage on her own. Perhaps she was missing Sophie even more than Clarissa had first thought.

'It looks like you're all finished, darling. Well done.' Lady Clarissa kissed the top of her daughter's head and pushed back her chair. She walked to the sideboard and pulled out the cutlery drawer. 'I just need to set the dining-room table and then I'll be right back.'

'Why are we eating in there?' Clementine asked. The dining room was usually reserved for guests and special occasions, like birthdays and Christmas.

'Well, it's a special occasion,' Clarissa said.

Clementine and Will glanced at each other and frowned. Drew opened the oven door and pulled out a large leg of pork nestled in among roasted vegetables. He placed the baking dish onto the bench and pierced the joint of meat with a long skewer.

At that moment Violet Appleby walked into the kitchen. She inhaled deeply and sighed. 'If that tastes anywhere near as good as it smells, Drew, I'd suggest you put a tenant into Crabtree Cottage and stay here permanently,' she declared.

Clementine's eyes widened at the thought.

'Do you need a hand with anything?' Aunt Violet offered.

'Goodness me. If I knew you were going to become such an enthusiastic assistant, I'd have asked Drew to move to the village months ago,' Clarissa teased.

'Everything's under control,' the man replied. 'I'll just get this back into the oven. I might even have a little surprise for you all later tonight.'

Clementine blanched. 'What surprise?'

'It wouldn't be a surprise if I told you now, Clemmie,' Drew said. He was pleased to see the child had regained her curiosity.

'I'd better get that table set,' Clarissa said.

'I'll help you.' Clementine hopped off her chair and followed her mother to the door, slipping her hand into Clarissa's.

The woman looked down and smiled. 'Are you sure everything is all right?'

Clementine nodded. 'I love you, Mummy.'

A crease ran across the top of Clarissa's nose. 'And I love you too, sweetheart.'

Clementine tightened her grip on her mother's fingers as the pair walked down the hall. Clarissa felt the warmth of her daughter's little hand in hers and felt like the luckiest woman in the world.

DESSERT DISASTER

Aunt Violet lifted her cutlery. '*Bon
appétit*, everyone.'

'That's French,' Clementine said.
She thought of Sophie and wondered what she
was doing at the moment.

'Very good,' Aunt Violet said with a smile.

'So what sort of treat are we in for on Friday,
Clemmie?' Uncle Digby asked.

'Just some boring songs Mrs Bottomley says
old people like and Saskia being the boss,'
Clementine replied. 'And I'm saying a poem.'

'That's wonderful,' Clarissa said. 'Why didn't you tell us?'

'I forgot,' Clementine said.

'What do you mean Saskia is in charge?' Aunt Violet asked. 'I thought you were going to be the host.'

Clementine shook her head. 'Mrs Bottomley chose Saskia because she has no grandparents,' the girl explained. 'And I muddled up my line.'

'Don't tell me that brat's managed to pull the wool over Ethel's eyes already,' Aunt Violet said. 'I'll have a word to her.'

'Please don't get involved,' Lady Clarissa said. 'Just because the child was a bit tricky with us doesn't mean she's like that at school.'

Drew nodded and passed her the gravy boat. 'She might be one of those school angels and home devils.'

'She was mean to Clemmie at lunchtime,' Will piped up.

'Oh, darling, really?' Clarissa reached out and patted her daughter's arm. It explained why she had been out of sorts when they had picked her up from school. 'Do you want me to say something to Mr Smee?'

'No! I can look after myself,' Clementine insisted.

Clarissa smiled at her. 'I know you can.'

'I'm going to give Will's grandparents a call tonight and see if they can come along too,' Drew said.

'Why don't you ask them to stay for the weekend?' Clarissa suggested.

'Meeting the parents, hey?' Uncle Digby said, popping a piece of pumpkin into his mouth. Clarissa's face blushed a deep shade of red.

'Well, why not?' Drew said, grinning.

Clementine bit her lip.

'I must say, Drew, I like the way you've glazed this pork,' Aunt Violet said. 'It's got quite the bite to it.'

'Yes, and this crackling is superb – although I'd better not break a tooth,' Digby joked. 'It's good to have another man in the house who knows his way around the kitchen.'

'Speaking of which, I've got a little surprise,' Drew said.

Clementine, who had been reaching for a glass of water, gasped at the mention of a surprise. Her arm shot out, sending the glass flying across the table. Digby Pertwhistle was out of his seat in a flash and raced off to the kitchen, bringing back a couple of clean tea towels to mop up the spill.

'Sorry, Mummy,' Clementine said, just as the shrill ring of the telephone sounded.

'I'll get it,' Lady Clarissa said, hurrying from the room. She was gone for quite a while before she returned looking rather flustered.

'Is everything all right?' Drew asked.

'I'm afraid we're about to get a lot busier,' Clarissa said. 'I've just had a booking for a group of ladies who are coming to take art lessons in Highton Mill for the rest of the week. They had reservations at another place but apparently there was a mistake.'

'How many are in their group?' Digby asked.

'Eight,' Clarissa replied. 'And I know we

have some other bookings later in the week too. I'm sorry, I had thought things were going to be quiet.'

'Don't apologise, Clarissa,' said Drew. 'It's much better to be busy, and Will and I don't require any looking after.'

'Certainly not. You're practically family,' Aunt Violet said. 'You know, when that happens, it's all downhill from there. You'll be hard-pressed to get anyone to make a cup of tea for you.'

Drew smiled. 'You know I'm very happy to make my own tea.'

Once Uncle Digby had cleared the plates and made a trip to the kitchen, Drew hopped up. 'I'll be back in a minute,' he said mysteriously.

'Where are you going?' Clementine asked.

'Yeah, what are you doing, Dad?' Will said.

'You two are such little stickybeaks,' Drew laughed. 'You'll see. It's a *surprise*.'

Clementine looked at Will. She wondered if he was thinking the same thing she was.

'So, Will, what do you think of Ellery Prep?' Uncle Digby asked.

'It's good, mostly,' the boy replied.

Digby Pertwhistle nodded. 'It's always tricky being new.'

Aunt Violet rolled her eyes. 'How would you know that? You've had the same job your whole life!'

'Okay, eyes closed, everyone,' Drew called from the hallway.

Clementine shut her eyes and put her fingers over the top. But she couldn't bear it and spread them apart a tiny bit.

There was a small pause followed by fumbling before Drew spoke up again. 'Clarissa, will you –'

Clementine gasped and leapt out of her chair. She rushed to the door just as Drew walked through it. The little girl crashed straight into him and the towering confection he was carrying flew into the air, showering pastry missiles all over the room. Uncle Digby lunged forward with his arms outstretched, skilfully catching profiteroles in both hands. Aunt Violet wasn't so lucky. One smacked

against her forehead, leaving a giant splodge of yellow custard dripping down her nose. Will's mouth fell open and Clarissa's eyes were the size of dinner plates.

'Clemmie!' Clarissa scolded. 'What did you do that for?'

Clementine looked back at the mess, her eyes filling with tears. 'I'm sorry,' she blurted, then fled across the entrance foyer and up the stairs. She ran into her room and hurled herself onto the bed, sobbing into the pillows.

TO THE MOON
AND BACK

By the time Will tapped on Clementine's bedroom door, the girl's racking sobs had calmed to shuddering sniffles. 'Are you okay?' Will asked as he sat down beside her. Lavender was sitting on the floor, staring up at her mistress.

Clementine rolled over. 'Is Mummy very cross?' she asked, her voice wavering.

Will shook his head and passed her a tissue. 'It's all fixed and they're eating now.'

'Really?' Clementine's blue eyes shone like crystal pools. 'I didn't mean to ruin your dad's dessert. I just . . . panicked.'

'Did you think he was going to ask your mum to marry him?' Will asked.

Aunt Violet had walked upstairs and was about to head into Clementine's room when she heard the two children talking. She stopped just outside the door.

'He said he had a surprise,' Clementine explained. 'And then he said, "Clarissa, will you?"'

'I know,' Will said, 'but I think he was just going to ask her to clear a place for the dessert.'

Clementine nodded. 'Anyway, you said he wouldn't marry Mummy.'

'I don't know that for sure. I was just mad because of Saskia,' Will replied sheepishly.

'Me too,' Clementine said. 'But what if she's right? What if they do get married and have a baby and they don't want us anymore?'

Violet Appleby listened carefully. 'Oh, those poor poppets,' she whispered.

'My dad loves me a lot and your mum loves

you a lot too. Maybe they would just love us twice as much,' Will said.

'My mummy says that she loves me to the moon and back and that's really far,' Clementine agreed.

'My dad says he loves me times infinity, which means forever,' Will said.

'So they could love us to the moon and back times infinity.' Clementine smiled and looked at the boy. 'I wouldn't mind if you were my brother.'

'Me either,' Will said. He leaned over and hugged her.

Violet Appleby poked her head around the door just in time to see the pair embrace.

'You're a really good listener,' Clementine said, hugging him back.

Aunt Violet dabbed at her eyes, then blew her nose, alerting the children to her arrival. 'Is everyone all right in here?' she asked.

Clementine and Will turned around and nodded.

'Good. Now, Clemmie, you mustn't be worried. Your mother is not in the least bit

upset, although Drew's dessert looks like it's been hit by a bus – or perhaps trampled by a small child in a hurry – it still tastes delicious,' Aunt Violet assured her.

Clementine managed a tiny smile.

'Yes, and one other thing.' The old woman paused and stood in front of the children. 'No matter what happens in life, your parents will never stop loving you. It's just what they do.' She turned around and hurried out into the hallway, catching a little sob in her throat before it had a chance to escape. Then she rushed into her own room and closed the door behind her.

'Do you want some smashed dessert?' Will asked Clementine, holding out his hand.

Clementine grinned and placed her hand in his. 'Okay.'

The children hopped off the bed and walked back downstairs. Clementine stopped at the first-floor landing. 'That's Granny and Grandpa,' she said, pointing at the portraits on the wall. 'They're really good listeners too.'

BETTER DAYS

With a houseful of guests and end-less rehearsals for Grandparents' Day, the rest of the week sped by. Clementine had recited her poem perfectly on every occasion. Saskia, on the other hand, kept making up new lines and adding to her part, much to Mrs Bottomley's displeasure.

Life in the classroom had improved a lot too. Clementine hadn't said a thing to Mr Smee about Saskia, but when she arrived at school on Tuesday, the teacher had already moved the girl to sit with Astrid. Clementine was glad, especially as she now got to sit with Poppy instead. Astrid didn't tolerate one second of Saskia's nonsense. When she caught the girl copying her work, she dobbed her in right away. Mr Smee warned Saskia that, if she continued looking at Astrid's work, he'd let Mrs Bottomley know to find another host for the Grandparents' Day. That appeared to be enough of a threat to keep the girl in line for a little while.

Clementine had begun her first letter to Sophie, but was planning to finish it on the weekend and add some photographs as well. She and Will were back to their usual happy selves, and there was only one thing they were waiting for. But there had been no announcement as yet.

On Friday morning, Clarissa and Drew accompanied the two children to school with a car boot full of cakes for the Grandparents' Day morning tea. Clarissa had been enlisted to help set up and serve the guests, along with a few other parents. Their special reward was being able to see the concert, as the hall wasn't big enough to accommodate parents and grandparents at the event.

'Is it just me or does this week seem like it's been going forever?' Clarissa sighed.

'You poor thing. You must be exhausted from looking after all those guests,' Drew said.

Clarissa shrugged. 'At least they were lovely. They enjoyed your lasagne last night, that's for sure.'

'Me too,' Clementine piped up from the back of the car.

'Dad, remember when you picked us up from school on Monday and you were going to tell us something?' Will said. 'What was it?'

Drew and Clarissa smiled at each other. 'We'll talk about it later,' the man replied, winking in the rear-vision mirror.

'I thought you two said you didn't want any surprises?' Clarissa teased.

'Monday was a bad day,' Clementine replied. 'But we're ready for a surprise now.'

'Are you just?' Clarissa's eyes twinkled. She and Drew had thought it best to save their announcement until the weekend, when they could celebrate properly and have time to answer the inevitable bombardment of questions.

Clementine clenched her fists in anticipation and Will raised his eyebrows, making her giggle.

'Look, there's Miss Critchley,' Clarissa said. The head teacher was standing by the gate and waving at them. 'I think she wants us to go to the teachers' car park.'

Drew turned into the driveway and found a spot. Miss Critchley, looking as elegant as ever in a pale pink silk blouse and navy trousers, hurried over to them.

'Miss Critchley's getting married in the next holidays,' Clementine said to Will. 'She was supposed to get married when I was in Kindy but they put it off for some reason. Do you know why, Mummy?'

'Miss Critchley's father wasn't well but he's

better now. She's going to be a gorgeous bride, isn't she?' Clarissa said.

'I know someone else who'd make a beautiful bride,' Drew said as he shut off the engine.

Clarissa blushed and shook her head. 'More like an ancient one,' she said quietly.

'Did you hear that?' Clementine whispered to Will as they clambered out of the car. 'I think they're talking about my mum.'

Will nodded and grinned. 'I think so too.'

The children said goodbye to their parents and dashed off to their classrooms.

ON WITH THE SHOW

thel Bottomley waved her arms about in an attempt to wrangle some additional volume out of the children. Most inconveniently, the sound system had suddenly packed it in. The rotten thing had worked perfectly all week until now. She'd sent Angus to tell Miss Critchley, who had been helping Drew and Clarissa to set up the morning tea. When the boy alerted her to the impending disaster of a hall full of elderly people and no amplification, Drew had immediately offered to help. He had followed cords all over the place, looking for a loose connection, and was still trying to unravel the mystery when the doors at the back of the hall opened. A man with a walking stick shuffled down the aisle to take up a seat in the front row.

'Who opened those doors?' Mrs Bottomley demanded, squinting into the light. She waited for her eyes to adjust so she could make out the culprit. 'You are far too early. We haven't finished our rehearsal yet.'

'That's bad planning then, isn't it?' the elderly gentleman quipped. 'You can't expect us to stand around outside. I've got a bad back, you know, not to mention a gammy leg and two dodgy knees. Don't even get me started on the hips! I can hula dance better than a Hawaiian teenager.'

The children giggled and a few began to swing their hips, pretending to do the hula.

'Yes, all right,' Ethel Bottomley harrumphed loudly and signalled for Mr Smee to draw the curtains across the stage. 'That's the end of that then,' the woman said, pursing her lips.

'Just do your best and sing loudly, children. I can't believe the sound system is on the blink today of all days.'

'Will the microphone be ready in time?' Saskia asked sweetly.

'I hope so. Mr Barnsley is looking for the problem now. Are you sure that none of you touched anything when we were in here yesterday?' The woman looked daggers at Joshua, who she'd noticed was fiddling with something while he was supposed to be singing the other day.

The children kept quiet as mice as the hall began to fill up.

'Saskia, don't forget that we've swapped some things around,' Mrs Bottomley reminded her. 'Clementine's poem is now part of the finale.'

The girl rolled her eyes and sighed impatiently. 'I know. I don't even need this,' she said, waving her script around. 'I learned it all off by heart last night. Clemmie Rose isn't the only one who can remember things.'

'Well, I'd rather that you had it with you. Perhaps it will remind you to not add in anything that isn't written in plain English,' the teacher said pointedly. She was beginning to regret her decision to allow someone as unpredictable as Saskia Baker to have such a big part in the proceedings.

The children could hear the crowd building from the other side of the curtain.

'Where's my grandson?' a man asked loudly. 'They said he'd be in the hall and there are no children here. Are they invisible?'

The children sniggered into their hands.

'There's a seat just here, Mavis,' another man could be heard shouting.

'What treat?' an old woman shouted back. 'Where's my treat?'

'Seat, dear. I said *seat*,' the man yelled.

Joshua snorted and the other children began to laugh all over again.

'Stop it, you lot,' Mrs Bottomley ordered.

Violet Appleby and Digby Pertwhistle walked into the hall together.

'Godfathers, did you ever think we'd be part of *this* crowd?' The woman looked around and shuddered.

'At least we haven't got walking frames and hearing aids,' Uncle Digby sighed.

'What did you say?' Aunt Violet asked, before breaking into a grin.

Digby Pertwhistle raised an eyebrow. 'You're getting funnier in your old age, Vi.'

Violet straightened her shoulders. 'It's Miss Appleby to *you*, thank you very much. I've had enough of this Vi business from Mr Baker. Oh, look, there's Clarissa. I wonder who she's with.'

The pair walked over to find Clarissa chatting to a well-dressed couple. The man had white hair while the woman's bob was a glossy chestnut colour.

'Hello Aunt Violet, Uncle Digby,' Clarissa said. 'May I introduce Drew's parents? This is Mr and Mrs Barnsley.'

'Please call us Ida and Charles,' the woman said. 'It's so lovely to finally meet you both. Drew's talked about you all with such affection.

We'd only seen him for a few minutes when he introduced us to Clarissa, but,' she said, lowering her voice, 'she's every bit as lovely as he's told us.'

Clarissa's face took on the same hue as the raspberry-coloured dress she was wearing. 'Why don't we find somewhere for you to sit?' she suggested. 'There's always a bit of a bunfight for the best seats and I think I can still see four near the front.'

The group scooted down the aisle. Aunt Violet sat beside Ida, who she decided within minutes was rather lovely. She was just about to ask the woman if she happened to play bridge when, all of a sudden, there was a tremendous kerfuffle at the back of the hall.

'Where's our star? She's had star quality ever since she was born,' the man declared, his voice echoing around the room.

'Good heavens, he's a bit enthusiastic, isn't he?' Ida Barnsley said.

Aunt Violet nodded and turned around to see a man in a gaudy plaid jacket and yellow trousers. The woman beside him wore a blue hat with a veil and a plume of peacock feathers that reached into the sky. They were heading straight for the front. 'Interesting fashion sense too,' Aunt Violet murmured.

The woman in the hat came to a stop in front of a mouse-like granny wearing a grey cardigan with pearl buttons. 'Excuse me, I think we're supposed to be sitting here,' she said loudly. 'Our granddaughter has the main part and our daughter said there would be seats in the front row.'

The mousy woman twitched nervously and apologised. She stood up and scurried up the aisle, leaving her seat and the spare one beside it.

'Do you think she's behind the curtain?' asked the woman in the hat. 'I wonder what she's wearing. I hope it's that lovely purple dress I got for her last Christmas.'

'Who's that?' Joshua said, prompting a round of shushes from Mrs Bottomley and the other children.

Saskia tore the corner of her script and kept her head down.

Mrs Bottomley glanced at her watch and searched the stage for Drew. She caught his eye, hoping for good news, but the man just shook his head. 'Right, children, time to get on with the show,' she said.

Saskia baulked. 'What about my microphone?'

'You're just going to have to use your loudest voice,' Mrs Bottomley replied. 'If Mr Barnsley manages a miracle in the next few minutes, we'll give it to you.'

Mrs Bottomley signalled for the children to stand and nodded at Mr Smee, who turned the house lights down and began to open the curtain. Mrs Wang's fingers burst into a flurry of activity, dancing along the piano keys as the children started to sing.

CONCERT CHAOS

The oldies were soon tapping along to the medley of songs that formed the first part of the concert. Mrs Bottomley's arms flew all over the place as she conducted the group. The children finished and took a bow, then sat down on the risers.

Saskia stepped forward. 'Good morning, everyone, and welcome to Grandparents' Day. My name is Sassy Baker and I'm the host for this morning's show. Today the children in Kindy, Year One and Year Two are going to perform a variety of items for your pleasure.'

The woman in the front row with the peacock hat waved. Her smile couldn't have been any wider. 'Hello Sass!' she trilled.

'Where's your microphone, darling?' the man beside her called out.

'I thought she said she didn't know any old people?' Poppy whispered to Clementine.

'Can you speak up, please? I can't hear anything down the back here,' a man in a cobalt cardigan yelled.

Saskia glared at him. 'Our next performer,' she yelled at the top of her lungs, 'is Astrid, who will read a story that she wrote.'

'You don't have to screech,' the man shouted back at her. 'I'm not deaf, you know.'

Astrid stepped into the centre of the stage and, in her best loud voice, read her story about a princess who slays a dragon. After the girl received lukewarm applause, Mrs Bottomley waddled back onstage and stood in front of the music stand. She tapped the baton on the stand, then turned to face the crowd. 'Good morning, everyone. My name is Ethel Bottomley and I am the Kindergarten teacher here at Ellery Prep.'

A woman squinted through thick glasses. 'Did she just say she has a big bottom?' she whispered. The people on either side of her began to guffaw. 'Well, she has, hasn't she? I can't see my Evie at all when she stands there.' The woman's lips disappeared into a tight line.

Mrs Bottomley gave the signal to Mrs Wang and the children began to sing again. Although a significant number of audience members couldn't hear the words, they hummed along to the tune and some even joined in at the chorus.

Meanwhile, out the back, Drew was out of ideas. He had searched high and low and couldn't find any logical reason for the sound system not working. He was about to give up when he noticed a cord running under the tiered seating that the children were on.

A boy was holding the end of it and fiddling with the plug. Drew waited for the next round of applause before he dived in behind them and gave the cord a good yank.

Joshua Tribble's head snapped in his direction. 'Hey, what are you doing?' he said.

'Give that to me!' Drew hissed.

Joshua wrinkled his nose and reluctantly parted with it. Drew hurriedly plugged it in and there was a loud *poomf* as the microphone came to life. He circled around the back of the children to hand it to Saskia, who was standing at the end of the second row.

'About time,' the child said, rolling her eyes. When the song ended, Saskia walked to the centre of the stage, microphone in hand.

Ethel wondered what had happened to her script and then noticed a pile of confetti-sized pieces of paper on the floor beside the second row. She dreaded what the child might be about to say.

'And now I have to introduce Clementine to do a poem for you, which she wrote.' The girl walked away but not before muttering, 'And it's really boring.'

'How dare she?' Aunt Violet grumbled. She had half a mind to march up onto the stage and drag the girl off.

Clementine bit her lip and looked out at the crowd. She spotted Uncle Digby and Aunt Violet and smiled. She then glanced sideways at her mother and Drew standing in the wings. They both gave her a thumbs up. Clementine took a deep breath and turned back to the audience. 'I wrote this poem about my mummy because she's the best mummy in the whole wide world,' she began.

Clementine recited the words perfectly. By the end, there were quite a few people reaching for their handkerchiefs and even Aunt Violet mopped at her eyes.

'Bravo,' the man in the ugly plaid jacket called out as Clementine took a bow. 'That was brilliant!'

'Oh, well done, sweetheart. You must be the apple of your mummy's eye,' said the woman beside him.

Saskia's face resembled a thundercloud as she stormed across the stage and snatched the microphone from Clementine's hand. 'She's not even your real mum,' Saskia scoffed.

The crowd gasped.

'Sassy, that's a dreadful thing to say!' the woman with the peacock hat called out. 'Apologise to that little girl right now!'

'No!' Saskia spat.

Clementine swallowed. She could feel her eyes beginning to sting.

Clarissa Appleby's heart was pounding as she watched her tiny daughter.

'I told you what's going to happen when your mum marries his dad,' Saskia hissed, pointing at Drew.

The audience sucked in another breath.

'Saskia May Baker, you stop that right now,' the man in the plaid jacket ordered.

'What's going on? I didn't hear what she said,' an elderly gentleman called. He had thin strands of long hair slicked over from one side of his head to the other.

'Excuse me, young lady, how dare you?' Aunt Violet stood up and marched towards the stage.

Clarissa and Drew looked at each other.

Will had made his way down from the risers and onto the stage behind Clemmie. Ethel Bottomley was flapping about on the edge of the wings wondering what she should do next.

'Clemmie and I want our dad and mum to get married,' Will said, smiling at Clementine.

Clarissa gasped. 'Oh my goodness, that explains everything.'

'The kids have been acting strangely because they thought I was going to propose,' Drew said, coming to the same realisation.

'Who's getting married?' demanded the gentleman with the slicked-over hair.

'No one's getting married,' Drew replied. He walked onto the stage with Clarissa by his side.

Clementine and Will exchanged quizzical looks. 'But what about your big surprise?' Clementine asked.

'What happened to the singing?' A lady in the second row peered around the peacock hat, trying to get a better view. 'Are the children doing a play now? I hope it's not Shakespeare – he's terribly boring.'

Clarissa smiled at the two children. 'Is that what you thought it was?'

Clementine and Will nodded.

'How do you feel about that?' Drew asked.

'Well, at first we were upset because Saskia said that you wouldn't love us anymore and you'd have a baby and it would be the most important thing,' Clementine explained.

Saskia stomped her foot. 'I never said that!'

'Sassy, that's very disappointing,' the man in the plaid jacket said, shaking his head.

'Well, she deserved it. She's got a pig and she's going to be on television, but *I* should be on television. I'm much prettier,' Saskia spat.

'Are they your grandparents?' Joshua called out.

'Yes, I'm Dodge and this is Fifi.' The man puffed out his chest.

'But she said her grandparents were dead,' Joshua cried.

'What?' Dodge's forehead puckered. 'Why would you say that?'

Saskia turned and glared at the boy. 'I didn't.'

'Yes, you did,' Joshua retorted.

'Are you telling lies again, young lady?' Fifi stood up and walked towards the edge of the stage.

Saskia glared at her grandmother. 'Stop being so mean to me, Fifi! You're always so mean and bossy. I wish you were dead!'

'Good heavens, that child is a fireball,' Aunt Violet said as Saskia hurled herself onto the floor, clenching her fists and thumping the stage. At that moment she couldn't help feeling sorry for her ghastly grandparents.

Clarissa put her arm around Clementine's shoulders. 'Of course we'll still love you no matter what happens – that's a special promise between every parent and their child.'

'Are you still upset about the idea of us getting married?' Drew asked.

Will and Clementine shook their heads. 'I want Clemmie to be my sister,' Will said.

'And I want Will to be my brother,' Clemmie added. 'But if that isn't the surprise, Mummy, what is?'

Drew nodded at Clarissa. 'We'd better tell them.'

'It seems I've won a trip to France! We're going to take you to visit Sophie in the next holidays,' the woman said. A huge smile spread across her face.

'Really?' Clementine beamed. Will did too.

As the children spun around, they were surprised to see Drew sink onto one knee.

'What are you doing?' Clarissa held her breath.

'Oh, is this *Romeo and Juliet*?' the woman in the front row said loudly. 'I really don't like that play at all.'

The audience craned their necks to see what was happening.

'Well, I had been saving this for when the time was right, but now that we know the children are happy, why wait?' Drew said. 'Besides, everyone we love is right here.'

Clarissa blushed and tears welled in her eyes as Drew pulled a small box from his pocket and popped it open, revealing a sparkling diamond ring.

'Clarissa Appleby,' he said softly, 'would you do me the honour of becoming my wife?'

'Oh, Drew,' she sighed. 'Yes.'

As he stood up and placed the ring on her finger, the audience clapped and cheered. Joshua Tribble whistled loudly.

'I told you they'd get married,' Aunt Violet said, grabbing Uncle Digby's arm.

Digby Pertwhistle chuckled. 'I seem to recall I predicted it first.'

'What happened? Is she in some sort of strife?' the old man in the cobalt cardigan called out.

'No, but I suspect that one there is about to be.' Aunt Violet looked over at Saskia, whose face seemed set to explode.

'Are they getting married?' Saskia blurted.

She pointed at Clementine. 'Will she get to be a flower girl?'

Clarissa nodded. 'Of course.'

Clementine's eyes lit up.

'But I want to be a flower girl!' Saskia thumped her fists on the floor. 'I'd make a much prettier flower girl than her!'

'Put a sock in it,' her grandfather ordered.

Mrs Bottomley nodded. 'I couldn't have said it better myself, sir.'

Clementine and Will hugged each other fiercely. The girl felt as though she might burst with excitement. 'France and a wedding!' she exclaimed. 'I can't wait to tell Sophie!'

But as the news sank in, her smile was replaced with a look of concern.

Violet Appleby glanced over at her. 'What's the matter, Clementine?'

Clementine clasped her hands together. 'I need to learn *lots* more French right away.'

Aunt Violet smiled. 'Oh, don't you worry about that,' she said with a wink. 'We'll get started this evening *tout de suite*.'

CAST OF CHARACTERS

Clementine Rose Appleby	Six-year-old daughter of Lady Clarissa
Lavender	Clementine's teacup pig
Lady Clarissa Appleby	Clementine's mother and the owner of Penberthy House
Digby Pertwhistle	Butler at Penberthy House
Aunt Violet Appleby	Clementine's grandfather's sister
Pharaoh	Aunt Violet's beloved sphynx cat

School staff and students

Miss Arabella Critchley	Head teacher
Mrs Ethel Bottomley	Kindergarten teacher at Ellery Prep
Mr Roderick Smee	Clementine's Year One teacher
Mrs Wang	Music teacher at Ellery Prep
Sophie Rousseau	Clementine's best friend
Poppy Bauer	Clementine's friend, classmate
Angus Archibald	Friend in Clementine's class
Joshua Tribble	Clementine's classmate
Teddy Hobbs	Twin brother of Tilda, classmate
Tilda Hobbs	Twin sister of Teddy, classmate
Astrid	Clever Year One girl
Evie	Clementine's classmate
Ally	Clementine's classmate

Friends and village folk

Margaret Mogg	Owner of the Penberthy Floss village shop
Pierre Rousseau	Owner of Pierre's Patisserie in Highton Mill
Odette Rousseau	Pierre's wife and Sophie's mother
Basil Hobbs	Documentary filmmaker and neighbour
Drew Barnsley	Friend of Clarissa's
Will Barnsley	Drew's seven-year-old son
Charles Barnsley	Drew's father
Ida Barnsley	Drew's mother

Others

Roger Baker	New baker at Pierre's Patisserie
Chanelle Baker	Roger's wife
Saskia Baker	Roger and Chanelle's six-year-old daughter
Dodge	Chanelle Baker's father
Fifi	Chanelle Baker's mother

LITTLE FRENCH WORDS

au revoir	until we meet again
bon appétit	enjoy your meal
bonjour	hello
derrière	bottom
ma chérie	my darling
merci	thank you
non	no
oui	yes
poulet	chicken
tout de suite	right away
très bien	very good

ABOUT THE AUTHOR

Jacqueline Harvey taught for many years in girls' boarding schools. She is the author of the bestselling Alice-Miranda series and the Clementine Rose series, and was awarded Honour Book in the 2006 Australian CBC Awards for her picture book *The Sound of the Sea*. She now writes full-time and is working on more Alice-Miranda and Clementine Rose adventures.

www.jacquelineharvey.com.au

JACQUELINE SUPPORTS

Jacqueline Harvey is a passionate educator who enjoys sharing her love of reading and writing with children and adults alike. She is an ambassador for Dymocks Children's Charities and Room to Read. Find out more at www.dcc.gofundraise.com.au and www.roomtoread.org/australia.

Look out for the next adventure

CLEMENTINE ROSE

1 July 2016